To Jake

From SANTA

It was Christmas Eve and Jake
was snug and warm in his cosy bed.
He was trying so hard to go to sleep,
but he could hear strange noises.

It wasn't the sound of sleigh bells.
It wasn't the sound of reindeer hoofs on the roof.
wasn't even the sound of Santa unpacking his sack.

It was more of a

HARRUMPH!

and an

OOF!

It was no use.

There would be no sleep for Jake
until he had found out what
was making that noise.

Jake crept down the stairs
and peered into the living room.
There were three stockings
hanging from the fireplace.

One of them belonged to Jake. But where had the other two come from? Suddenly, a muffled voice came from the chimney.

Jake

"Oh, dear. I'm even **more** stuck now!"

There was a scuffling sound
from behind the Christmas
tree, and Jake jumped
when a small elf appeared.

Jake

"Uh, hello," said the elf. "I guess you've caught us!"

Jake listened as the elf explained
that Santa was stuck in the chimney.
The elf had tried to pull him out, but the
only things that had come down so far
were Santa's boots and trousers!

"I can help you," suggested Jake.
"I'll hold Santa's feet and we can both pull."
The elf agreed. "Between us we might
be able to get him unstuck."

Jake firmly grasped both of Santa's feet.
Suddenly a light went on upstairs.
"Jake, is that you?" called his mum.
"Back to bed now, please, or Santa won't come!"

Jake

At that moment
Santa shot back up
the chimney... with
Jake still hanging
onto his feet!

The poor elf could not believe his eyes.
But there was no time to think…
Jake's mum was coming
out of her bedroom.

"I'm coming!" squeaked the elf. He hurried
up the stairs and jumped into Jake's
bed, pulling the covers over his head.
"Night night, sweetie," said Jake's mum.

Meanwhile, up on the roof, Santa and Jake had landed in a heap. The clever reindeer had hooked their reins under Santa's arms and pulled as hard as they could.

"Good work!" said Santa, brushing himself off. "No more mince pies for me tonight!"

Jake scrambled to his feet, but Santa was so busy that he didn't notice Jake and the elf had switched places!

"I think we had better deliver the rest of the presents first," said Santa, "and leave this house for last."

Santa climbed into the driver's seat.

"Elf, you get the presents ready
for our next destination,"
he called over his shoulder.
"But I'm not Elf..."
replied Jake.

Santa wasn't listening.
He was talking to the reindeer.
"Up, up and away!" Santa called,
and the reindeer took off before
Jake had time to explain.

Jake held on tight as the sleigh
soared high over the rooftops
and into the night sky.

Surrounded by sacks, Jake was
so busy working out which presents were
which that there was no time to let Santa
know a mistake had been made.

There were **big**
presents for the cities,

and **SHINY** presents
for the towns.

There were **ODD**-shaped
presents for the villages,

and **unusual**
presents for the farms.

To
Jake

As they landed at their next stop, Santa decided that he couldn't risk getting stuck in a chimney again.

"Elf, I think you had better make the deliveries from now on," Santa said. "I'll sort the presents."

Jake *shimmied* down chimneys.

He **squeezed** through cat flaps.

And, if all else failed, he used Santa's *magic* key to let himself in.

In each house Jake picked up the mince pies to take to Mrs Claus and carrots for the reindeer.

Finally there was just one sack left, and
Santa still hadn't realised his mistake!
The sleigh headed back over the
rooftops to Jake's house.

Sliding down his chimney with
a sack of his own presents was
the most fun Jake had ever had.

He put his presents under the
Christmas tree, then picked up
Santa's trousers and boots and
placed them in the sack.

Jake

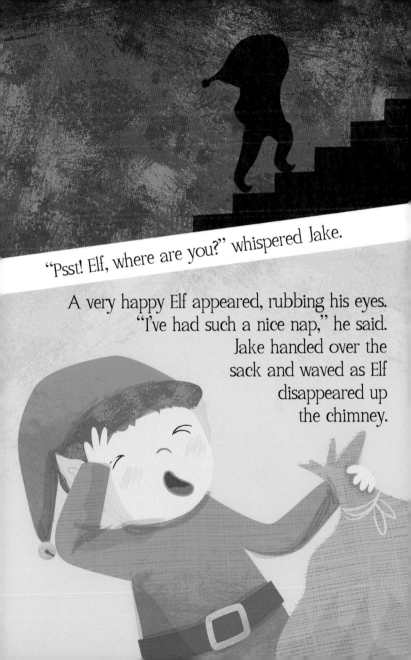

"Psst! Elf, where are you?" whispered Jake.

A very happy Elf appeared, rubbing his eyes.
"I've had such a nice nap," he said.
Jake handed over the
sack and waved as Elf
disappeared up
the chimney.

Back in his cosy bed, Jake could
hear the sounds of jingling sleigh bells,
reindeer hoofs on the roof and, very faintly,

"Ho, ho, ho!

Merry Christmas!"

Or was that,

"Ho, ho, ho!
Yummy mince pies!"?

Write your name on the labels.

Draw yourself as an elf.

Written by Katherine Sully
Illustrated by Julia Seal
Designed by Nicola Moore

This edition published by HOMETOWN WORLD in 2018
Hometown World Ltd
1 Queen Street
Bath
BA1 1HE

www.hometownworld.co.uk

Follow us @hometownworldbooks

Put Me In The Story is a registered trademark of Sourcebooks, Inc.

Copyright © Hometown World Ltd 2018

ISBN 978-1-78553-575-8
All rights reserved
Printed in Italy
HTW_PO201814

Bestselling books starring your child!

www.putmeinthestory.co.uk